CLASSIC STARTS™

Moby-Dick

*Retold from the Herman Melville original
by Kathleen Olmstead*

Illustrated by Eric Freeberg

STERLING

New York / London
www.sterlingpublishing.com/kids

STERLING and the distinctive Sterling logo
are registered trademarks of Sterling Publishing Co., Inc.

Library of Congress Cataloging-in-Publication Data

Olmstead, Kathleen.
   Moby-Dick / retold from the Herman Melville original by Kathleen Olmstead ;
illustrated by Eric Freeberg.
       p. cm. — (Classic starts)
   Summary: An abridged retelling of the adventures of a young seaman when
he joins the crew of the whaling ship Pequod, led by the fanatical Captain Ahab
in pursuit of the white whale Moby Dick.
   ISBN 978-1-4027-6644-2
   [1. Whaling—Fiction. 2. Whales—Fiction. 3. Sea stories.] I. Freeberg, Eric, ill.
II. Melville, Herman, 1819–1891. Moby Dick. III. Title.
   PZ7.O499Mob 2010
   [Fic]—dc22

                                                                2009004836

Lot#: 11/09
2   4   6   8   10   9   7   5   3   1
Published by Sterling Publishing Co., Inc.
387 Park Avenue South, New York, NY 10016
Text © 2010 by Kathleen Olmstead
Illustrations © 2010 by Eric Freeberg
Distributed in Canada by Sterling Publishing
^c/_o Canadian Manda Group, 165 Dufferin Street
Toronto, Ontario, Canada M6K 3H6
Distributed in the United Kingdom by GMC Distribution Services
Castle Place, 166 High Street, Lewes, East Sussex, England BN7 1XU
Distributed in Australia by Capricorn Link (Australia) Pty. Ltd.
P.O. Box 704, Windsor, NSW 2756, Australia

Sterling ISBN 978-1-4027-6644-2

For information about custom editions, special sales, premium and
corporate purchases, please contact Sterling Special Sales
Department at 800-805-5489 or specialsales@sterlingpublishing.com.

CONTENTS

CHAPTER 1

The Spouter Inn

✑

Call me Ishmael. Some years ago, I was in need of work. I had no plans for my life and no real home. So, I decided to go to sea and see some of the world. I had done this before. Whenever I feel a bit low or that life is too hard, I get work on a ship. Otherwise, I get too restless. I may find myself walking into the street and knocking people's hats off.

I doubt that I am the only man who feels this way. If you are in a city near the ocean, you will see hundreds of people gazing at the water.

I cannot understand how some can work in an office. I need freedom and the open sea or I would go mad.

Men like me cannot resist the pull of the sea. We would spend our last dime for a trip to the beach. We would walk through a desert to reach a shore. We are always happiest on a ship when there is no land in sight.

I never go to sea as a passenger, though. A passenger needs money to buy a ticket. A passenger gets seasick and complains about the service. No, when I go to sea, I go as a sailor.

I stuffed a shirt or two into my bag, tucked it under my arm, and headed toward the Atlantic Ocean. I arrived in the town of New Bedford too late. The last boat to the island of Nantucket was gone. I was very disappointed. I was determined to find employment on a Nantucket ship.

Nantucket whaling ships were the finest

heading out to sea. Nantucket was also the oldest whaling port in America. I wanted to be a part of that history and would not settle for second best.

Fishing for whales—called whaling—was a big industry back then. Whale blubber was used for oil in lamps. Everyone needed oil lamps to see at night. The oil was even used in street lamps. Hundreds of ships sailed each year looking for whales. They sailed all over the world and were gone for several years at a time. It was hard work, but I wanted to know that adventure.

The next boat to Nantucket didn't leave for another two days. I knew no one in New Bedford. I would need to find a place to stay and something to eat. So, I walked toward the water where cheaper hotels would surely be found.

At last, I found the Spouter Inn. The sign

said the owner was named Peter Coffin. The building was leaning to one side. The old sign creaked loudly in the wind. It certainly didn't look like a nice hotel, but it looked perfect for me.

The inside of the hotel was almost as run-down as the outside. The wallpaper was worn and faded. The furniture was tattered. It reminded me of the insides of a condemned ship.

On one wall there was a large oil painting. It was so dirty and damaged by years of smoke that you could not tell what the picture was. It appeared to be a black mass over another black mass. I stared at it for some time. I finally realized it was a picture of a whale, the great monster of the deep.

The opposite wall was covered with har-poons and spears. These are tools that a whaler uses. I wondered what stories these tools could tell. Where had they traveled? Which whalers had used them?

I walked through the dusty lobby. There were more display cases with treasures from far-off lands. I stopped in my tracks when I looked into a side room. There was a whale's jawbone. It was so large that a horse and buggy could have passed through.

I was still staring in amazement when a very old man entered the room. I told him I was looking for a room before I traveled to Nantucket.

"You don't have any objections to sharing with a harpooner, do you?" he asked. "If you're going whaling, you'll have to get used to it anyway. That *is* why you're going to Nantucket, isn't it? For whaling?"

"I don't really like sharing a bed," I said. "But if that's all you have and the harpooner is a decent fellow . . ."

"Good!" the landlord said. "Do you want

supper? It will be here in a minute."

He walked out of the room. I was left alone with my thoughts. I wondered what would happen next and what might be served for supper.

CHAPTER 2

A New Roommate

⌒

In no time at all, I was sitting down to supper. It was a very good meal with meat and potatoes and dumplings. It was the first good meal I'd had in a long time.

I looked at the group of men around the table. Were any of them my mysterious roommate? When I asked the landlord, he shook his head.

Just then, a group of very loud men entered the inn. It was the crew of the *Grampus*. The ship had just landed after a three-year voyage.

They were all noisy and excited as they ate and drank. I sat in silence, listening. They put on quite the show while talking over one another. I was very entertained.

After dinner, I waited in the lounge area with the landlord. I was still curious about my missing roommate.

"Where could this man be?" I asked the landlord. "Does he always stay out this late?"

"Oh, no," the landlord said. "He's usually in early and up early. I guess he's having trouble selling his wares."

"His wares? What do you mean?" I asked.

"Trinkets. Beads and treasures and the like that he's brought back from voyages," the landlord said. "This town is full of such stuff, though. Too many sailors trying to sell things."

"Do you think he's still trying to sell them at this hour?" I asked. It was already midnight.

"Hard to say," he replied. "He's never been

this late. Might not return at all, I suppose."

With that, we decided it was time for bed. The landlord took me upstairs to the room and let me in. The bed was quite large and would certainly fit two men comfortably.

I was still wary about sharing the bed with a strange man but decided the landlord was right in guessing he was gone for the night. Even though I was quite tired, I tossed and turned for some time before falling asleep.

Then, just after drifting off, I was awoken by footsteps in the hall. I lay quietly in bed as the door opened. A large man stood in the door frame. He walked in and set his candle down in the corner of the room.

I said hello so he would know I was in the room. He did not reply.

When he turned to look at me, I saw his face in the candlelight. My word! I had never seen anything like it. At first, I thought he had been in a fight. His face looked blackened and bruised. It took me a moment to realize they were tattoos. Black squares of ink decorated his entire face.

He took off his fur cap and laid it down. When he took his shirt off, I saw that his body was covered in the same tattoos.

I thought of escaping through the window, but we were on the second floor. Also, I was not a coward. I had never seen a man like this before, but that was no reason to be afraid.

That is, until he started to attack me! He suddenly jumped onto the bed. He began to push and poke at me. I struggled to get free.

"Who are you?" he grunted. "Tell me who you are!"

I called for the landlord. "Peter Coffin! Come quickly! This man is attacking me." In only a few moments, the landlord was at the door with his candle.

"There's no need for this fuss," the land-lord said. "Queequeg won't harm a hair on your head."

"Not harm a hair!" I shouted. "Look at him! He is trying to hurt me!"

But even as I said the words, I noticed that Queequeg was sitting back quietly against the wall. He was smiling to himself. I started to feel embarrassed that I had caused such a disturbance.

"I'm sorry that you were surprised by Queequeg," the landlord said. "I thought you understood he was a native from New Zealand. He's a good fellow. He won't try to scare you again. Will you, Queequeg?"

"No," the harpooner said. "No more trou-bles. Now get back to bed," he said to me. "It's time for sleep."

I quickly realized that I had been unfair. I had made too many quick judgments about this man. He put on a show because he knew I was frightened by his appearance. He had no intention of hurting me.

We both turned in and I never had a better night of sleep in my life.

CHAPTER 3

The Chapel

I woke up the next morning feeling rested and refreshed. Queequeg woke up at the same time. I watched him wash at the basin, then dress. He put on his waistcoat and hat. Then, taking his harpoon, he left the room without a word.

I followed him shortly after.

All the other guests at the breakfast table were whalers. This time, they all sat quietly and ate. I thought this was very funny, as sailors were known to be loud and talkative. Perhaps that was only when at sea or just back from a long voyage.

Queequeg sat at the head of the table. He ate nothing but meat. No rolls. No butter. Just meat.

After breakfast, everyone went into the parlor. I went outside for a stroll.

I had never been to New Bedford before. I was surprised by all the different people. There were men of almost every color, and people seemed to wear whatever they wanted. One man wore a beaver hat, a fancy waistcoat, and a wide belt with a knife stuck down one side.

I made my way to a chapel. I am a Christian but do not make it to church every Sunday. It is hard to keep a routine when I'm at sea so often.

The sermon was just about to start. I sat down among sailors, sailors' wives, and sailors' widows and waited.

All around the chapel, there were plaques. These signs were put up in memory of sailors who had died at sea. They were donated by their families and shipmates.

I looked to my left. I was surprised to see Queequeg sitting down the row from me. I knew that he was not a Christian. He carried a little pagan doll with him that he prayed to. I had seen it with him in the hotel room.

Queequeg nodded when he saw me. He then went back to waiting patiently for the sermon to begin.

The minister walked to the front of the chapel. Father Mapple was an older man. He was very tall and had a mane of wild gray hair. He was well-known as a former whaler and harpooner. I had heard talk of him from other whalers before I arrived.

Father Mapple climbed a ladder to reach the pulpit. He did this slowly and with dramatic flair. When he reached the top, he dragged the ladder up. Now no one could climb up and he could not climb down. He looked like a sailor in the crow's nest, high atop the mast of a ship.

Father Mapple called the room to order. "Gangway to starboard! Midships! Midships!" He was using the language that sailors use on a ship. He was telling the crowd to move in from the sides and take their seats.

Just as Father Mapple began to speak, a terrible storm started outside. Wind and rain whipped against the windows. The minister was not bothered, though. His voice was calm and strong. No one else was bothered about the weather, either. They were only concerned with Father Mapple's words.

He told the story of Jonah in the belly of the whale. "You know it from the Bible," he said to the crowd. "You've heard the story, but have you listened to the words?"

He recounted how Jonah did not want to follow God's wishes. He tried to escape by ship.

When terrible storms arose, the crew realized it was Jonah causing the problems. He was thrown overboard and swallowed by a whale.

Jonah did not pray for immediate delivery. He knew that his punishment was just. He had sinned and needed time in his whale-prison. He knew that he would be saved if God believed he deserved it. The minister wanted everyone to understand that if they did sin—and they should try not to—they should repent like Jonah.

The men in this chapel understood how frightening a whale could be. They all had faced the beasts many times. Father Mapple reminded the whalers to ask God to forgive them when they sinned. That was how Jonah was saved from the belly of the whale.

When I returned to the Spouter Inn, I found Queequeg sitting before the fire. He was flipping through the pages of a book. Every fifteen pages, or so, he stopped and looked around the room.

This gave me a chance to look at him more closely. I realized at that moment that there was no hiding of the soul. He might be covered in black tattoos—something very strange to me—but you could plainly see that he had a simple, honest heart.

As we both sat there, Queequeg said nothing to me. In fact, he acted as though I was not in the room. I thought this strange considering we had been roommates the night before. Was that not worth a nod to say hello?

It occurred to me that I had not seen Queequeg talk with any of the other men, either. He seemed to keep entirely to himself. So, I decided that I should make a friend of him.

I pulled my chair up to his bench. I recalled what had happened the night before, and how frightened I had been when he entered the room. This made Queequeg smile a bit.

He asked if we would be roommates again. When I said yes, he seemed pleased.

"Can you read?" I asked. I pointed to the book in his lap.

He shook his head no.

I then explained to him the text of the book—it was about whaling, of course—and our conversation came quite easy after that. We talked about the sights around town and the places we had traveled.

After some time, Queequeg hugged me and pressed his forehead to mine. He called us buddies.

"I will die for you," he said. He slapped me on my back. "If it must be, I will die for you."

Now, for my countrymen, that was an odd thing to say so shortly after meeting someone. For Queequeg, though, it was a social custom. To him, it did not seem strange at all. So I did not consider it strange, either.

He also wanted to share with me all his material goods. He took out thirty dollars in silver that he had in his pocket. He divided this in two and gave me half. I tried to say no but he would not listen. He simply dropped the coins into my trouser pocket.

Queequeg told me about his home. He came from Kokovoko, an island far to the west and far to the south. It is not on any map. True places never are.

He said he had a wonderful childhood. His father was a tribal chief, and Queequeg was in line to take over one day. He loved his home but wanted to see more of the world. When an American whaling ship docked in his harbor, he decided to join the crew.

Over the years, Queequeg attempted to fit in. He wore clothes like his shipmates. He talked in their strange language. He even tried to follow their Christian religion, but he couldn't quite do it. He found that they said one thing then did another. For this, he decided to stay a pagan.

I asked him if he considered going home soon.

"No," he said, shaking his head. "I worry that I have changed too much to go home. Your Christian world is very different from mine."

Then he asked what brought me to New Bedford. I told him that I had decided to try my hand at whaling. I had been to sea many times but never on a whaling ship. My next destination was Nantucket to find work. Queequeg said that he would accompany me. He would get work on the same ship and we would stay together. I was very happy to hear this.

CHAPTER 4

The Voyage to Nantucket

~∽

The next day, Queequeg and I checked out of the Spouter Inn. We carried all of our belongings in a wheelbarrow down to the dock and booked passage on a boat to Nantucket. I very soon saw the troubles that Queequeg faced being so different.

Many of the other passengers on board were very rude to him. They called him a lot of hurtful names. Some of them even called me names. They seemed bothered that we were friends. Queequeg was angry that they spoke to me this way, but he did his best to ignore them.

However, when one young man tried to prove himself by pushing Queequeg, my friend took action. Queequeg picked the man up in both his arms. He lifted him high above his head.

The man thought Queequeg was going to throw him into the water. He started to scream, "Put me down!"

Queequeg carried him to the side of the crowd and set him on top of a stack of boxes. Until that moment, I had not noticed that Queequeg was quite tall. The young man was stuck high above the deck. His friends had to come over and help him down.

The man then caused a great deal of fuss. He called to the captain, claiming that he was in danger. He claimed that everyone was in danger because my friend was a threat.

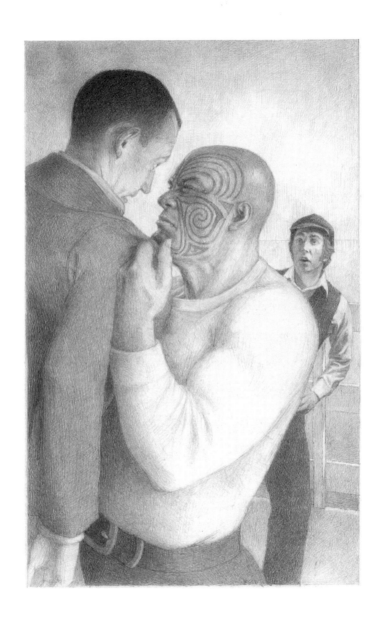

The captain, seeing Queequeg's tattooed face, believed the young man. He started to yell. Queequeg, who simply stood quietly at the rail of the boat, looked out over the water. He remained calm and refused to look at any of them. I was proud to know such a patient man.

While the captain and his crew were occupied by calling Queequeg names, they did not notice the mast of the boat. It was under a great deal of strain. The ropes holding this heavy pole in place were tied too tight. When one of them snapped, the pole began to swing wildly across the deck.

No one seemed to know what to do. The crew stood and watched the mast swing out of control. It moved back and forth across the deck. The ropes that had held it in place dragged along with it, whipping wildly through the air. The crewmates were afraid they would be knocked overboard if they got too close.

And that was exactly what happened. A man moved in to get a closer look. He realized too late that this was a mistake. The beam swung back around and he was sent flying overboard.

Queequeg sprang into action. He found another rope and quickly tied it around the beam. He stopped it from swinging by bracing himself on the deck and holding tight. Then he ducked under the beam and tied the rope to the other side of the deck. It was now held in securely in place.

Then Queequeg took off his jacket and shirt and dove into the water. He swam around the boat for some time looking for the man. He had no luck, though. The man was gone.

When he returned to the deck, everyone was very grateful, especially the captain. They all tried to apologize for calling him names, but he brushed them aside.

Queequeg walked back to his place at the rail and continued to look out at the sea. He did not want to talk to anyone. He only wanted to be left alone.

CHAPTER 5

Nantucket

ᥫᩬ

Nantucket is a unique place. I have never seen another like it. It is a place made for sailors. I am almost sure that everyone who lives there is a sailor. Or is married to one. Or is a sailor's widow. When you live in Nantucket, the sea is your home.

We arrived late in the evening. Mr. Coffin, the landlord at the Spouter Inn, had recommended his cousin's hotel called the Try Pots. This was the name of the large kettles used on whaling ships to prepare the whale oil. This hotel was in better shape than Mr. Coffin's. We had a delicious supper of clam chowder and cod and made our way to our room.

We started to make a plan for the next day. Queequeg insisted that I be the one to find the ship. He said that's what his gods told him.

I did not think this was a good plan. I'd never taken a job on a whaling ship before. How would I know if I found the right one?

"Queequeg, you have much more experience than I do," I said. "We should look together. I trust your opinion."

Queequeg shook his head. "You must do it yourself," he said.

I knew there was no point in arguing. I resolved to set out the next day and find the best ship possible.

After another good night's sleep, I made my way down to the docks. I looked at the list of vessels shipping out. I had no way to determine which might be better than the other. I decided to investigate the *Pequod* because I recognized the name: It was the same name as a tribe of Native Americans.

I went to the ship to find the captain. If he seemed like the right man, then I would sign us on to join the crew.

The captain was not on board. Instead I found another man named Peleg. He was in charge of hiring the crew and buying all the supplies. I told him that I was looking for work.

"You're not from Nantucket, are you?" he said. I am not sure how he knew. It must have been his instincts.

I told him no. "This is my first time on a whaling ship," I said. "I've been to sea many times, though."

"There's nothing like a whaling ship," he told me with a scowl. "It makes no difference that you've been to sea before. Have you ever seen Captain Ahab?"

"No," I said. "Who is that?"

"Why, he's the captain of this ship," he said. "He's the captain of the *Pequod*! When you see him, you'll understand why whaling is different. Captain Ahab has lived the hard life of a whaler. He has suffered a great deal. Captain Ahab only has one leg."

"One leg!" I exclaimed. "How did that happen?"

"He lost it to a whale!" Peleg said.

In fact, Peleg almost shouted this. I was a little surprised by his energy. He was very excited.

"This is a very dangerous business," Peleg said. "Are you prepared to get close to a whale? So close that you can throw a harpoon into the whale's side? Will you be brave enough to fight against the waves and water as the whale rolls against your boat? As it tries to dive back under the ocean? You have to be willing to give up your life—or maybe your leg—to work aboard a whaling ship."

I realized that Peleg was trying to scare me, but it did not work. I am not easily frightened. I only saw this as a challenge.

"I am ready for it all," I said.

"Very well, then," he replied. He signed me up then and there.

"I also have a friend who wants to sail," I said. "He's a very experienced harpooner. He knows what to expect."

Peleg said I should bring him back with me.

Later that day, Queequeg and I signed our employment papers. Captain Peleg was impressed with all of Queequeg's experience. He said he was happy to hire him as a harpooner.

Afterward, we walked along the pier. A man in very dirty clothes and rumpled hair came up to us. I had never seen him before.

"Are you sailing on that ship?" he asked. "The *Pequod*?"

I told him yes and he began to laugh.

"Have you set your eyes on Old Thunder yet?" he said.

"Old Thunder?" I asked. "Who is that?"

"Why, Captain Ahab, of course," the man said. He laughed again. "Did they tell you all about your new captain?"

"What is there to tell?" I asked. This man annoyed me. I like people to be direct and say what they mean. He was speaking in riddles.

"There is plenty to tell," he cackled. "There are so many things that you should know."

"We know about his leg," I said. "We know that he lost a leg to a whale."

"Oh," the man said. "You know all about it, do you?" He laughed once again then started to turn away.

"I'll leave you to your new ship and captain,

then," he said.

"If you have something you want to say, then say it," I shouted after him.

"No," the man said. "You've signed your papers so there's no turning back now. I'll leave you to your own doom. I wish you the best of luck."

CHAPTER 6

The *Pequod*

⌒

The next few days were spent preparing the *Pequod* for her voyage. Sails were mended, food was brought on board, and the whole ship was checked for leaks. The *Pequod* would be gone for three years, so we had to be very prepared.

Then, one morning, as we approached the *Pequod*, we saw men walking along the deck of the ship. They were not regular crew members. They were wearing officers' jackets.

At this point we met Starbuck, the first mate. We also learned that Captain Ahab was aboard

the ship, and that we would set sail the next morning. We all worked hard to finish the preparations. We did not see the captain, though. He did not leave his cabin.

The next morning, we raised the anchor. The *Pequod* moved very slowly from the dock. The ship creaked and sighed as it pulled away. We seemed very sluggish in the water, as if we would never leave. For a brief time, I thought that our three-year voyage would end in the first ten minutes. All of the crew rallied together, though, and we made it into the harbor.

At this point, Peleg made a short speech. He was not going to travel with us. He was only going as far as the harbor before heading back to Nantucket.

"Good luck, men," he shouted. All the crew was gathered on deck. "You're heading out for a long voyage, but you're in good hands. Captain Ahab will lead you well."

Peleg then gave orders to the men on deck. Starbuck should keep an eye on the supplies. Stubbs should keep the sails in good repair. Flask should watch for weak spots in the ship. Then Peleg climbed down to a small boat at the side of the *Pequod* and headed back to shore.

I soon became an admirer of Starbuck, the first mate. He was a tall, quiet, and sensible man. He was born in Nantucket and had a great deal of experience on whaling ships. He saw it not as a great adventure, like others did, but as hard work. For Starbuck, his was a job that required care and respect. He often said, "If a man is not afraid of a whale, I do not want him on my ship."

I did not understand this until after my first whale hunt. Then I learned that if a man thinks he can do anything when fighting against a whale, he puts everyone in danger. He must always be cautious. Starbuck put the safety of others first. He was not interested in impressing people.

Knowing these things about him, as I do, it makes it hard to tell this story. Starbuck was a good man. I worry that you might not think well of him when you learn this entire tale. I hope you will remember that I admired him a great deal.

Stubbs was the second mate. He was a happy-go-lucky man who did his job, but never more than was expected of him. Nothing seemed to bother him. His mood was the same if we were in a terrible storm, fighting a whale, or sailing in calm waters. There was no difference.

Flask was the third mate. He was gruff and grumpy. Flask was very capable in his job but seemed to find no joy in it. He did not marvel at the wonders of the sea. He did not consider the whale a majestic beast. It was just something he needed to capture. Nothing more, nothing less. The fact that the whale did not want to be captured only made him grumpier.

When a whale was in sight, the *Pequod* would send out four boats with a small crew in each. We were told Captain Ahab always led one. Starbuck, Stubbs, and Flask would take charge of the other boats. They each had their own harpooner and a crew of men to row.

Starbuck chose Queequeg to be in his boat. Since he was first mate, he had first pick, and he knew that Queequeg was the best harpooner on board.

Several days into the voyage, we still had not laid eyes on Captain Ahab. I was very curious to see him. The strange man on the dock had stirred my interest about "Old Thunder." Every time I was on deck, my eyes scanned for someone new. I looked for Starbuck, thinking Ahab might be with him. I had no luck. The captain remained in his cabin.

It was almost a week into our voyage before I finally saw the captain. One evening, I was called to watch on the upper deck. When I turned around to look over the ship, shivers ran down my back. Standing at the very front, gazing at the sea, was Captain Ahab.

He looked like a statue carved from stone. Strong, firm, and solid. His skin was tanned and leathery from so many years in the sun. Along one side of his head was a long white scar. I never learned where this scar came from, or if it was old or new. Members of the crew sometimes guessed about how he had received this mark, but no one knew for certain.

I was greatly affected by the sight of the captain. He was a grand figure. It took me several moments to notice that he had a peg made of ivory where one leg should be.

He stared straight out to sea, lost in thought. He did not speak. He did not pay attention to the other men on deck. No one spoke to him. Captain Ahab looked like a man very troubled by what he saw, but I could not tell you what that was. I could see only endless water.

Ahab stayed on deck for a short time before leaving. He slowly climbed back down the ladder, moving his ivory leg slowly down the rungs. He returned to his cabin without saying a word.

CHAPTER 7

Captain Ahab

～

After that evening, I saw Ahab every day. He continued his silence but came out to inspect the ship and watch the water daily. As time went on and the weather improved, so did Captain Ahab's spirits.

When warm winds arrived in April and May, Ahab began to act more like the rest of the crew. He even seemed to enjoy our company. There were times when he had a faint blossom of a look that—on any other man—might have flowered into a smile.

As we traveled south on our trip around the world, the weather grew warmer. It was pleasant to be on deck, enjoying the sun. Even Ahab preferred the open air to his cabin. He seemed to be regaining his strength and his spirit. "Going down to my dark cabin feels like going into my own tomb," he said once.

The captain was not a young man. Perhaps it was hard for him to go up and down the ladder, especially with his ivory leg. If so, he would not admit it. We could only hear it in his breath as he occasionally struggled during the climb.

The captain spent a good deal of his time pacing back and forth across the deck. He walked from one side to the other, scanning the sea. Everyone below could hear the *tap-tap-tap* of his ivory leg on the wooden deck. It was a near-constant rhythm, and it seemed to help him keep his routine. He was looking for something out in the waters. I imagined that it was something more than just a whale.

You might think that life on the *Pequod* was unruly. Sailors—especially men who work on whaling ships—can be rough and tough. But we must follow rules like everyone else. In fact, life on a whaling ship is well ordered. We all have our place.

The captain, of course, is in charge. Everyone on board must do as he says. If not, we will be punished. We might be forced to do extra chores. Or we might lose our chance to go ashore or have time off. The captain has ultimate power on a ship. We must all obey his command.

After the captain, the mates are in control—Starbuck, then Stubbs, and then Flask. These were the officers of the *Pequod*. And as with officers on all ships, they ate and slept separate from the crew.

On a whaling ship, there is a slight difference

in the treatment of the crew. The harpooners are treated like officers. Harpooners have one of the most important jobs on a whaling ship. They are the ones who actually capture the whales with their spears. Therefore, they receive special treatment.

Even though Ahab was a moody man, he was not rude. He treated everyone with the same amount of respect and always demanded respect from his crew. He was simply odd in his habits.

We followed the same routine with each meal, at Ahab's request. The steward would call Captain Ahab to the table. At first, the captain would not respond, as if he did not hear. Then he would swing around and say, "Mr. Starbuck. Dinner." The captain then went below deck to the dining area.

Starbuck would wait a few moments until he was certain that the captain was sitting down.

He would then make a slow tour across the deck and say, "Mr. Stubbs. Dinner."

Stubbs, the second mate, would then do the same. Walking past the third mate, he would say, "Mr. Flask. Dinner." Stubbs then went below.

Flask, having no one left to call, always seemed much less stern as he went to his meal. In fact, he seemed almost happy. But as soon as he got to the door, he put on a more serious face. The moody captain would never appreciate so much cheer.

Ahab ruled over his dinners like a silent, but wild, sea lion. He paid very little attention to the other men at his table. They all watched him with much interest, but he only focused on eating. He cut his meat with a large knife and ate in silence.

When the officers finished, the table was cleared. Then the harpooners were brought into the cabin for their meal. This was remarkable because all the harpooners were natives. In most other places, certainly anyplace on land, a non-white man would never be allowed to eat and sleep where a white man does. But life at sea is different from life on land.

CHAPTER 8

Moby-Dick

Just after the warm weather started, I took my first turn in the masthead. The masthead is a lookout that sits high on top of a pole (also called a mast). The lookout is shaped like a bucket, and it's high above the deck so you can see far out to sea. Standing so high above water allows you to view things from a great distance. This meant we could see whales in faraway waters and direct the ship toward them.

I was up in the masthead for a while when I heard a great deal of noise on the deck. The captain was calling everyone to him. Even those of us on watch were called to gather around him.

We all stood on the main deck while Captain Ahab stood on the deck above. He was pacing back and forth, as usual, talking to his mates. He looked very excited.

Then Captain Ahab turned to talk to us. He held up a large gold coin.

"This," he said. "This is a sixteen-dollar coin. A doubloon!"

We all watched him with much curiosity.

"Any man who first sights the white-headed whale with a wrinkled brow and crooked jaw—and we bring him in—will win this doubloon," he said.

All of the men were excited. A few shouted out words of support.

"Keep your eyes out for white water," Captain Ahab said. "If you see bubbles, give a shout. If

you see a spout of water, call everyone to deck. We are looking for the white whale. Wherever he is in the sea, we will find him!"

"Is this the same whale they call Moby-Dick?" one of the harpooners asked.

"You've heard of Moby-Dick?" Ahab asked. He was astonished.

"Does his tail wave madly when he dives back underwater?" asked another man.

"Does he have old corkscrew-shaped harpoons stuck to his side?" Queequeg asked.

"Yes!" Ahab said. "Yes, you've described him perfectly. So, you've seen him. You've all seen Moby-Dick!" The captain was very excited.

Some men said they had seen him. Others said they had only heard stories. Everyone began to tell his story of the white whale. Ahab paced back and forth again across the deck. He was shouting to each of them. "Yes, yes!" he would say. "That is the devil. You speak of Moby-Dick!"

Nobody had ever seen the captain act so wildly. Ahab was usually a moody and quiet man. Starbuck looked concerned that something might be wrong with his captain.

"Sir," Starbuck said. It took him several tries to get Ahab's attention. "Was it Moby-Dick that took your leg?"

Ahab calmed down. He stopped pacing across the deck and put his hands behind his back. He looked at Starbuck with great sadness. "Yes," he said. "It was Moby-Dick who crippled me."

The captain quickly became troubled again. "Aye!" he shouted. "Yes! It was the white whale that crippled me so! He did this to me and he will pay. I will chase him all over the globe! I will chase him until he is mine."

Ahab turned to his men again. He walked to the edge of the upper deck and leaned against the rail. We all stood below him, watching his every move.

"And you men will help me!" he shouted. "This is why we have shipped. You will sail with me through all the seas of this earth until we have captured that white whale. We will not stop until he is no more!"

The harpooners and crew all cheered. We were up to the challenge. We all supported our captain in his quest. Everyone, that is, except Starbuck.

"Why do you look so serious?" Ahab asked him. "Are you not up for the task of finding Moby-Dick?"

"I am happy to take him down if he crosses our path," Starbuck said. "But I do not want him taking us from our jobs. We signed on to hunt whales. We are looking for whale oil. We are not here to hunt your personal enemy."

"I know things you do not," Ahab said quietly. His voice was almost a hiss. "I have been in the mouth of this whale. He took my leg. You do not understand and you cannot tell me otherwise. If you try to defy me, it is rebellion!"

Starbuck shook his head. He knew there was no arguing the matter with his captain. "It is madness," he said under his breath before turning away.

All the men continued to cheer. The captain had excited them with this challenge and promise of reward. "Death to the white whale," they shouted. "Death to Moby-Dick!"

Ahab encouraged the men for a while—enjoying the excitement—before sending everyone back to work. The high spirits continued, though. Only Starbuck was quiet. Only he seemed to be worried about our new mission.

CHAPTER 9

Planning the Hunt

For days—for weeks, even—after Captain Ahab's announcement, the men talked of little else. Many of the men were excited to hunt for the white whale. Some were nervous about it. No one wanted to say anything against Captain Ahab. Only Starbuck ever disagreed with the plan. However, even he said nothing more to the captain about Moby-Dick.

I was fully with the captain in his quest. His excitement inspired me. His need for revenge excited me. I felt like it was my mission, too.

The white whale was well-known to whalers. Many had heard of him, but few had laid eyes on him. And many who said they had seen him were only telling tall tales. Many men wanted their own Moby-Dick story to tell. I was no exception.

Moby-Dick was known for his size and his anger. He was much larger than other whales. This white whale was known to smash ships and send sailors to watery graves. He lashed harpooning boats with his tail, breaking them into splinters. There were so many of these tales that it was hard to know what was truth and what was rumor. Moby-Dick was seen all over the world, often at the same time! Everyone wanted to have an encounter with him. Everyone wanted to be part of the legend.

And here I was at sea with a man who'd had a real and terrifying experience with the whale. He was looking for Moby-Dick again to put an end to his life. As a member of the *Pequod* crew, I would be a part of this great event.

At night, Captain Ahab studied his navigation charts. He sat in his cabin, bent over his table, examining his maps. An oil lamp, held up by chains, swung above his head. It kept the same rhythm as the waves.

It might seem like an impossible task to search for one animal—however large—in all the oceans of the world. It did not seem impossible to Ahab, though. He knew all of the tides. He knew the yearly path of the whales. He knew where and when the whale's food traveled. He knew many stories of the white whale by heart. He knew when and where it was seen. He was certain that all this information would lead him to Moby-Dick.

Much like humans, whales are creatures of habit. They stay on the same routes. Ahab was certain that he could find the whale and was obsessed by this goal. He spent every waking hour plotting the course. He studied all of his charts. There was never a moment when he did not think about the white whale. Every day was the same.

I started to wonder if searching for Moby-Dick might be too much for our captain. I wondered if all this worry and concern would drive our captain insane.

CHAPTER 10

The Hunt

One sunny, quiet afternoon, Queequeg and I were working on deck. It was not difficult work. We were weaving mats to use in the harpooning boats. It was a simple task, and we were enjoying our time together.

Suddenly this peaceful moment was disturbed by shouting.

"Avast!" the voice cried. "There she blows!"

We all rushed to the side of the ship to see the whale. It was enormous! My heart began to beat wildly as I watched it swim past. I was surprised that something so large could move so gracefully.

Water shot from its spout. We then saw the others. Whales travel together in "pods" and this pod was large. They all swam in a group not far from our ship. Each person rushed to take his post.

The three mates—Starbuck, Stubbs, and Flask—quickly got into their whaleboats. These small wooden vessels were about twenty feet long. Each one had a single sail that helped it gain speed while men rowed after the whale.

Their harpooners and rowers jumped in with them. There were usually about eight to ten men in a boat, including the six men rowing. After they all piled in, the boats were lowered down the side of the ship into the water. Captain Ahab got into his boat with his men and we all took after the whales.

The boats took their turns heading into the pod. Each harpooner had to get close enough to throw his spear. There was much shouting back and forth among the boats. It was hard work rowing around these enormous beasts. We all had to be on the lookout. The whales rolled on their sides and dove under water, sometimes taking a whaleboat with them.

When a boat was in place among the whales,

the men raised their oars so they stuck up straight into the sky. This kept them out of the way of the harpooner's view. It also meant they were ready to drop the oars and row together at a moment's notice.

I was in Starbuck's boat with Queequeg, enjoying the action. We had the first good shot at the whale. I was filled with excitement and I held my breath as my good friend prepared himself.

Starbuck shouted to Queequeg. "Now," he called. "Now is the time!"

Queequeg stood up and held the harpoon above his head. With great strength he threw it at the whale.

The harpoon sailed through the air and over the water. I felt as though time stood still. It seemed to take a long time to reach its target. Queequeg remained perfectly motionless, his muscles tensed. His arm stayed in midair as he waited to see where the harpoon landed. It missed and sank into the water.

A rope is attached to the end of each harpoon. If the harpooner misses the whale, he can pull the harpoon back to the boat. That was what Queequeg did. He pulled his harpoon back and quickly prepared himself for another shot.

Again, he stood up in the boat. He was remarkably steady considering how rough the waves were. They were at least ten feet high. Queequeg was perfectly focused on his job. He held his harpoon high above his head and again pitched it at the whale.

This time, the metal blade of the weapon hit the great beast, but it did not stick. The whale began to roll just as the spear was in the air. It skimmed past the whale and entered the water again. We were all disappointed but could not think about it for long. We soon faced a more serious matter.

The whale's tail began to thrash about. A stormy wave of water crashed onto our small boat. This wall of water left the boat unharmed but sent all the men overboard.

We swam around our boat looking for oars and any other tools that had been tossed into the water. It was difficult to swim against the giant waves, but we needed to save what we could. We were also facing a new problem. The weather was getting worse. The weather can change so quickly at sea. The sky was suddenly covered by a thick fog. Soon a storm would be upon us.

The wind was picking up. It was cold in the water. We tried to signal to the other boats but had little luck. It would be difficult for them to see or hear us in this rising storm. We could not see or hear them, either, so we had no way of knowing if they were near or far. We tried to climb aboard our little boat but it was too difficult. I was starting to worry that we might not all have the strength to hang on.

Just then, the *Pequod* came into view. For a brief moment, I thought she were going to run us over, but the crew saw us in time. Another of the whaleboats was signaled, and we were all pulled aboard. I watched as one by one my crewmates were pulled from the water.

I was the last one dragged back onto the *Pequod*. I do not think I have ever been so cold in my life. Queequeg was there to help me. He handed me a warm blanket.

"Does this happen often?" I asked. I was shivering so much that it was hard to speak. "Are you often tossed into the sea while trying to capture a whale?"

Queequeg nodded and smiled. "Yes," he said.

"It is pretty common."

He then slapped me on the back and went back to his work weaving the mat. He acted as though nothing had happened. I realized that I had better learn to do the same.

CHAPTER 11

Sightings

One moonlit night, off the coast of Portugal, we spotted a line of bubbles along the water. This was a sign that there was a whale—or many whales—just below the surface. Whales are mammals, and they breathe air. The bubbles were a sign that they were breathing out.

The man in the masthead spotted them first. He called, "There she blows!" The men, once again, ran into position.

We were too late, though. By the time Captain Ahab made it to the rail of the *Pequod*, the whale was gone. We all went back to bed disappointed.

Only a few nights later, bubbles appeared along the surface again. There was a spout of water as a whale reached the surface and exhaled air through its blowhole. A fountain of water shot into the sky. Again, the watchman in the masthead yelled, "There she blows!"

We all moved as quickly as we could. Once again, just as we were ready to go after it, the whale disappeared.

Some men insisted these sightings were the same whale. They insisted it was none other than Moby-Dick. Some even believed the whale was taunting us. They believed he was challenging us to a fight.

Captain Ahab, of course, was among this group. He believed the white whale was teasing him. We could often hear him mutter under his breath.

Starbuck was starting to believe that the captain was going insane. He was too focused on the white whale. He spoke of nothing else. Ahab did not talk about his wife and child at home. He did not talk about how many whales they had caught on the voyage. He was not concerned about how much oil they would bring home. He only cared about finding Moby-Dick. For Captain Ahab, there was nothing else.

Whenever we caught up with another ship, Ahab yelled across to them, "Have you seen the white whale?"

If there were no sightings, he would become angry. He would pace back and forth across his deck for hours at a time. He would mutter to himself and occasionally wave his fist in the air.

If there was a sighting, Ahab became very excited. He studied his maps closely, plotting exactly where we should go next. He constantly looked for food that a whale would eat. He knew that Moby-Dick would follow the same path.

It was our lucky day when we sailed into a mass of brit. *Brit* is the name we sailors use to describe a cloudy group of tiny fish. This is something that whales feed on. It was a good sign that we would see whales soon. We decided to stop traveling and wait for the whales to arrive.

Only a couple of days later, a great white mass was spotted in front of us. Dagoo, one of the harpooners, spotted it first.

"There!" he shouted. "Look there! The white whale! It's the white whale!"

Whenever someone gives the call that a whale is in sight, we move quickly. This time, however, we moved at lightning speed. No one wanted to miss this opportunity. We did not want to lose the white whale.

In a few minutes, we were all in position again, and the four boats were lowered into the water. Ahab's boat led the rest.

We spotted the creature right away. He was enormous. His body was vast and pulpy, and he rose to the surface near our boats then swam under.

My heart was beating fast. I could not believe that we were so close to Moby-Dick! After so much talk—and so many stories—we were finally going to capture the white whale.

I was surprised that he was so calm. All of the stories I heard were of him breaking boats with his tail and sending sailors overboard. This creature rose to the surface then sank again. He was gentle. He did not seem to even notice the boats surrounding him.

"It's not our whale," I heard Starbuck say quietly.

No one else in our boat heard him. We were all so focused on the white creature beneath us. Queequeg was standing up with harpoon in hand. He was waiting for our boat to get close enough so he could throw his spear.

"Not Moby-Dick?" I said.

"It's another monster of the deep," Starbuck said. He looked at me across our whaleboat. "The giant squid. Few men have seen it. Many people believe they are the largest creatures in the sea. Certainly, this squid here is just as frightening as our white whale. It might even be as dangerous as Moby-Dick."

"But it is not Moby-Dick," I said.

Starbuck shook his head slowly. I wondered if he was disappointed that it was not the white whale. Was that why Starbuck was so calm? Or was he relieved that it was not Moby-Dick?

I then noticed that Ahab, without saying

a word, turned his boat back to the *Pequod*. He must have realized that it was a squid, too.

When we returned to the ship, Ahab was already in his cabin. He did not come out again for another three days.

CHAPTER 12

The Line

⌒∽

Throughout this long tale of mine, I have described the many duties of a whaling ship crew. I have told you about meals and mending sails and mats. I have told you about harpoons and harpooners. I have described chasing whales in boats and the danger of being knocked overboard. But I have yet to describe the use of ropes. This may seem like a small matter, but it is very important.

A sailor uses rope for almost any job on board the ship. We have dozens of different knots that

we use for different jobs. One of the most important times rope is used is after a whale has been
killed.

We need to use great lines of rope when
pulling in the massive beasts. When the whale is
alongside the ship, it is secured with chains and
ropes. A whale could be as long as the ship—or
longer! So this is a very difficult task.

Ropes are tied from one side of the ship to
the other using rails and masts for support.
These crisscrossed lines are high above the deck.
Men perch on top of these woven ropes. As the
whale gets pulled in, the ropes must be constantly tightened and adjusted. If you're not very
careful, the whole ship could sink under the
whale's weight.

It is very dangerous work. Not only is it hard
to stay in place as the ship rocks with the weight
of a whale, but it is very dangerous to fall. You
could hit the deck from such a height, and

you could also become tangled in the ropes on your way down. More than one sailor has been hanged in this way.

Rope is one of our most important tools, so we treat it with respect. We always leave the rope just as we would like to find it. This is especially important when we are in a great rush.

For instance, when we are coiling a rope for the harpooner, we make sure it is prepared properly. We leave it in a circle, the rope stacked on itself as we wind it around. This keeps the rope free of knots. It also means that when the harpoon is thrown, the rope can follow easily behind it. Nothing will block its way. There will be no tangles or obstacles.

When you are a sailor—especially when you are on board a whaling ship—you must be prepared for any emergency. Things can change in an instant. When you are hunting a whale, you

must react quickly. You cannot be concerned about where to find a rope. Everything must be ready to go!

It was a part of our daily routine. We checked to make sure the rope was ready. We made sure that each of the whaleboats had its oars and lines and buckets to bail out excess water. This was how we started each day.

And so, it was a day like almost any other when I climbed the masthead to start my shift. It was warm. The slow roll of the waves and sun bouncing off the water was very soothing. I looked into the distance over the water and was quickly lost in my dreams. Suddenly I spotted bubbles and a spout of water.

There was a giant whale rolling in the waters near the *Pequod*. When it breathed out, water spouted far into the air. It was a beautiful sight. It was a shame that this was the end for this fine creature.

I gave the call, "There she blows!" Captain Ahab called everyone into the boats, and we were off again.

All four boats scrambled to get beside the whale. It was a frantic time. Stubbs and his team went in for the kill. He called for his men to wet the lines. This meant that the ropes were getting too hot from all the strain. Stubbs's men dropped water over them to cool them down. There was always the danger that the ropes could burst into flames.

Stubbs's harpooner sank his spear into the whale's back. The whale struggled for some time until its heart gave out.

The *Pequod* pulled in close. We all worked—the men in our boat and the crew on the *Pequod*— to drag the whale to the ship. We then pulled the whale apart to store its meat and oil for later. We had to do this fairly quickly, because sharks were always swift to come and feast.

Captain Ahab was not as excited about the catch as the rest of us. I think this whale reminded him of another. He was thinking too much about Moby-Dick, and this put him in a foul mood.

CHAPTER 13

Tying a Whale to a Ship

❦

When a whale is tied to the side of a ship, it has to be cut up slowly and carefully. Whaling ships are gone for a very long time. Whalers always hope to capture many whales. The more whales you get, the more oil you will have to sell at the end.

It would be impossible to bring a whole whale on board. They are simply too big. So we have to tie the whale to the side of the ship and cut it up. Then we take the oil and the parts we need and store them on the ship. A whaling ship is often at sea for several years. The oil can be stored in the giant tank or barrels on the ship all that time without spoiling.

It is the job of the harpooners to do most of the cutting. They are experts with knives. Also, the work can be dangerous. Harpooners just seem less worried about the danger. Perhaps this is because they are used to it.

With the whale chained to the side, each harpooner ties a rope to his belt and dangles from the side of the ship. The ropes get strapped to a beam that is attached to the railing and hung out over the water. This gives the harpooner a lot of room to move over the beast. Another crew member stands in the ship near this beam to help guide his harpooner's rope. Each harpooner has his own guide; they work as a team.

The harpooners swing back and forth through the water while carving pieces of the whale. They send pieces of meat back up to the ship.

There are many dangers associated with this task. The harpooners could easily smash against the side of the ship. They could also get tangled in the rope and trapped under water.

Queequeg and I were a very good team. He trusted me to hold tight and guide his rope well. I trusted him to move confidently and judge his distances properly.

He also had to stay very aware of all the sharks in the water below. Having the dead whale close to the ship brought in sharks looking for a meal.

There is one more problem with cutting up a whale, and you may have thought of it already. A whale is a very heavy creature. This, of course, means that the ship might lean to one side under all this weight.

One time when we had a whale attached to

the side of the *Pequod*, we were tilted so far over that we had to climb across the deck to the high end. In order to get to the other side, we had to pull ourselves along using the masthead as a step. Anything that was not secured to the deck slid down to the low end.

In whaling, this happens occasionally, and the captain usually has to make an important decision. Do you risk damaging your ship? Or do you let the whale go?

In this instance, though, Ahab did not make the decision. He was too preoccupied with his charts and maps to focus on what was happening at that moment on the *Pequod*. His mission to capture the white whale was far too important!

Starbuck made the call to cut the rope and let the whale go. He ordered Queequeg to use his knife to cut through the line. Some of us stood by the side of the ship as the giant sank slowly into the deep ocean.

It was sad to think that this magnificent beast had been killed for no reason. Unfortunately, though, this was just one of the harsh truths of whaling. It was not an easy job.

CHAPTER 14

Gabriel

ᴄᴏ

One day, we caught sight of a ship. As we approached it, Captain Ahab signaled to the crew. It was a common practice among sailors to stop and greet one another. It was one of the ways that news and mail were passed during long voyages.

This ship, however, did not come any closer to ours. Ahab demanded that the *Pequod* move in closer until we were a couple of dozen feet away. From that distance, Captain Ahab could talk easily with the men on the other ship.

Their captain—called Captain Mayhew—walked to the rails. We were told that many people on board his ship were very sick. They did not want to spread any germs. Therefore, they did not want us to get too close.

"I just want to know," Ahab called. He was shouting across to the other ship. "Have you come across the white whale?"

"Ah," said Captain Mayhew. "Moby-Dick. We know him well." Captain Mayhew then started telling his long tale.

"We had just shipped out of Nantucket when we found the wreck of another ship," he said. "It had been attacked by Moby-Dick. There was very little of it left."

Ahab was excited by this news. He was not upset to hear that men might have been hurt or killed during the attack. He was just happy to hear a report of the white whale.

"One of the men on my crew," Captain

Mayhew continued, "started to warn us about this great danger. Gabriel said we should stay away from the white whale. If we should see him, Gabriel said, we should sail the other way."

"And did you listen?" Ahab asked.

Captain Mayhew shook his head. "It was years later when we did find him," he said. "He was spotted from the masthead, and we went straight for him. How could we resist? Everyone knows about Moby-Dick. Everyone wants to be part of the crew that brings him in."

"But the whale won," Captain Ahab said. "Didn't he?"

This time, Captain Mayhew nodded. "We got into our boats and took chase. But the whale rammed one of our boats. One of our oarsmen was thrown. He landed forty feet away in the deep ocean. We never saw him again."

"And that was the last you saw of the white whale," Ahab said. Once again, he showed little concern for the man killed.

"All my men believed Gabriel. They think he was right all along." Captain Mayhew added, "We should never have looked for the white whale."

We all wondered what Captain Ahab would do with this news. This was a frightening story. We knew it would be dangerous trying to capture Moby-Dick. This story reminded us that one or more of us might face the same end as the man lost to the sea.

"Why do you ask these questions?" Captain Mayhew asked. "Are you still seeking the white whale?"

Ahab nodded. "Aye," he said.

Just then a man with red hair and a tattered waistcoat ran toward the rail of Captain Mayhew's ship.

"No!" he shouted across the water to Ahab. "You must stay away from the whale. He means doom to any man!"

"Gabriel!" Captain Mayhew said. "It is not your place to speak. You cannot talk to a ship's captain with that tone."

"But he needs to know!" Gabriel shouted. "Hunting the white whale will mean the end to him and all his crew!"

Ahab ignored these shouts. He would not even look at Gabriel. He did not have time for a madman.

"Captain Mayhew," Ahab said. "I believe we have a letter for one of your crew." Ahab sent Starbuck down into the hold to check the mailbag.

It was common for whaling ships to carry mail with them in case they ran into other ships. It was one of the only ways letters arrived over such long distances.

When Starbuck returned with the letter, Ahab read the name to Mayhew. "It's for a Harry Macey."

"Oh," Mayhew said with a sigh. "That's our man who was thrown from the boat."

"I'm sorry to hear that," Ahab said.

"We'll take it anyway," Mayhew said. "It seems like the right thing to do."

"No!" Gabriel shouted. "You should keep the letter. If you're seeking the white whale, then you'll soon be with Macey. You can give it to him yourself when you see him!"

Starbuck tried to pass the letter over to Mayhew using a long pole. Gabriel grabbed the pole and pushed it back. The letter fell back into the *Pequod* and landed at Ahab's feet.

Ahab was about to respond when the other ship turned suddenly. It picked up speed and was well on its way.

Gabriel had ordered the oarsmen to leave right away. Then, without confirming these orders with their captain, the crew left.

All of us on the *Pequod* were shocked to see

this behavior. Only a captain could give such orders. It appeared that Captain Mayhew did not demand the respect he deserved. Perhaps he, too, believed that Gabriel had special powers.

Perhaps the crew members all believed that following Gabriel and his orders meant they would never have to see the white whale again.

CHAPTER 15

The *Jungfrau*

∽

One day, we came upon another ship called the *Jungfrau*. We did not have to approach her and call out. She came right up beside us.

The crew was very anxious to make contact with the *Pequod*. As soon as the ships were close enough, the *Jungfrau* dropped a rowboat into the water. The captain rowed over to us.

"What's that he has in his hand?" Starbuck asked.

The captain was carrying a small tin. He held it up high while his men rowed. It looked as though he was trying to keep it safe.

"I think it's a lamp," Stubbs said.

And so it was! The captain was carrying an oil lamp to the *Pequod*.

"My word!" Starbuck exclaimed. "They've run out of oil! They're a whaling ship hunting for prey and they've run out of whale oil. Does that mean they have no whales in their hold?"

Everyone on deck shook their heads in amazement. They must have been at sea for many months without catching a whale.

As soon as the captain—named Derick, we found out—climbed on board, Ahab approached him. He wanted to know if the *Jungfrau* had seen Moby-Dick.

Captain Derick tried to answer Ahab, but he did not speak English well. The *Jungfrau* was a German ship. He struggled with the words but eventually made Ahab understand. They had not seen the white whale.

Captain Derick explained that he needed to refill the oil can. We let him, of course, then he headed back to his own boat.

He was almost back at the *Jungfrau* when we all spotted a group of whales. The captain of the *Jungfrau* did not even bother getting out of his rowboat. He passed the oil can to a man on deck and took off.

Boats from both ships quickly dropped into the water. The chase was on!

There were eight whales—an average-size pod. The creatures knew they were in danger. They swam close together, bumping into one another. It was difficult to get our boats close enough.

All the mates from the *Pequod*—Starbuck, Stubbs, and Flask—shouted to one another and to their crews.

They spoke in rough tones. They called one

another dogs. They taunted one another to row harder. It was all meant as encouragement, though. They were pushing the others to work harder. It was all a part of the game, the challenge to get to the whales first. They wanted to beat the German boat.

Captain Derick made too many mistakes. He was rushing to the whales and not concentrating on everything that he needed to do. His oars were getting caught in the waves. He could not keep up with the boats from the *Pequod*. With so many waves and all the excitement, his small boat almost flipped over.

That was when we took the lead. Without thinking or worrying about it, our men moved the boats into position. In no time all four of our boats had one of the whales surrounded.

The whale was in a terrible state of fright. It thrashed about and tried to get away, but we held our position. At the last moment, the harpooner in Derick's boat was about to fire, but he missed his chance. All three of our harpooners stood up almost in a straight line. They shot their harpoons.

Their spears darted over the heads of the Germans and made a perfect landing in the whale's back. In all the excitement, Derick's boat was knocked to the side. The captain and his harpooner were cast out into the sea.

Everything else happened very quickly.

Our men held on to the rope and pulled as tightly as they could. The whale made terrible sounds. It was so heavy that we were all afraid that the rope would break. We held on, though. The whale breathed its last breath, and we went about our business of dragging it back to the *Pequod*.

CHAPTER 16

Another Report of Moby-Dick

‿߷

We arrived in the waters south of Singapore while the weather was still good. Ahab was certain this is where he would finally battle the white whale. These were the waters in which he was most often seen.

We certainly found many whales there. Ahab was right that it was a feeding ground. We gave chase—this is how a sailor refers to a whale hunt—to them all.

By this time in our voyage, I could barely remember when I was not a whaler. I could barely remember the time before I joined the crew of the *Pequod*. I was so used to this hunt. I had learned to react with the instincts of someone who'd had years at sea. I loved the action and the adventure.

But there were always unexpected dangers. More than once, our tiny boats were trapped between two massive whales. It was only through Starbuck's excellent work that our boat ever escaped.

Not long after our run-in with the *Jungfrau*, we came upon yet another ship. This one was from England called the *Samuel Enderby*. We saluted her crew. They saluted us and invited us on board their ship.

Before leaving the *Pequod*, Ahab asked his usual question—had they encountered the white whale? The English captain didn't respond. He held up his arm instead. It was a fake arm made from whalebone.

"Aha!" Ahab cried. He quickly climbed into the boat and made his way to the other ship.

Unfortunately, he forgot that it would be difficult to climb onto an unfamiliar ship with his peg leg. The *Pequod* was specially equipped to help the captain get around. So, his climb aboard the English ship was a bit slower than expected.

When he finally reached the English captain—it seemed to take forever—Ahab asked about his arm.

"It was the whale, wasn't it?" he asked. "The whale took your arm?"

"Aye," the Englishman said. "Just as the whale took your leg."

Ahab nodded. "Tell me your tale," he said. "Describe your fight."

The Englishman nodded, then started his story.

"It was my first time out on a whaling ship. We were sailing smoothly one day when the ocean floor seemed to rise up beside us. It was the great white whale. I had not heard of him before. He had a giant white head and wrinkled brow. There were old harpoons stuck into his side."

"Those were mine," Ahab whispered. It almost sounded like a hiss. "Those were my harpoons."

"He was trying to bite our fast-line," the Englishman continued.

"Yes," Ahab said excitedly. "I know him! I know that is what he does. But go on! Tell us the rest."

"I am trying," the Englishman said.

Ahab tried to settle down but it was difficult. He longed to hear stories of the whale.

"As I said," the Englishman continued. "The whale was biting on a line we had tied between our two boats. His teeth must have stuck on the line but we didn't know it.

"So when we tugged down on it, he was pulled on his side and we were all tossed clean into the air. And where should we land? Right on his back! The whale made another few quick dashes and our tiny boat was destroyed.

"I tried to hang on to a harpoon sticking out of his side but that did not last long. The sea around me was too strong, and I was pulled under. On my way down, my shoulder caught on another harpoon sticking out of the whale. It tore my flesh open."

The ship's surgeon then joined the conversation. He told the men all about his attempts to save the captain's arm. The injury was too great, though. They had to cut it off.

All the men listened to the story carefully, but Ahab was growing impatient. He did not want to hear about the captain's recovery. He wanted to know about the whale.

"Did you see him again?" he asked. "Is that

the last time you saw Moby-Dick?"

"We weren't even sure if it was Moby-Dick," the Englishman said. "As I said before, I was new to whaling ships at the time. It wasn't until we met other whalers and compared notes that I knew it was him."

"But have you seen him again?" Ahab insisted.

"Yes," the Englishman said. "Twice more."

"And you didn't catch him," Ahab said. He sounded astonished.

"We didn't even try," the Englishman said. "I've lost one limb. That's enough."

"You must remember," the ship's surgeon interrupted, "a whale cannot digest anything large. It is physically impossible. If one bites you, it is only because of its own awkwardness."

With that, Ahab could wait no longer. He threw his hands in the air and let out an impatient sigh.

"Back in the boat, men!" he hollered to his oarsmen. In no time flat they were back at the *Pequod*.

When he arrived back on the ship, Ahab took a good look at his ivory leg. It became obvious that he had done some damage to it. He was not used to so much thumping and rushing about. He had become too agitated at the story of the whale and probably had stamped his leg without realizing it. Ahab called over the carpenter.

"I want you to make me a new leg," he said. "Use a piece of whalebone that we have in storage. Find the best piece and get all the fittings ready. I will need it by tonight."

The carpenter left immediately to find the perfect piece of whalebone for his captain.

CHAPTER 17

Starbuck

こう

While Ahab was in his cabin, plotting his maps and waiting for his new leg to be completed, the rest of us went about our jobs. We had to pump the whale oil into barrels. These barrels were to be stored in the ship's cargo hold.

Starbuck was directing the men in the hold when he was called back up to the deck. One of the men had noticed that oil was leaking into the waters around the *Pequod*. This was not a good thing. There was a leak in the barrels.

Starbuck went to the captain's office to talk

to Ahab about this new problem and I followed in case there were new orders.

"Sir," Starbuck said. "We're leaking oil out of the hold. We'll have to stop in Japan for repairs."

"Stop?" Ahab said. "Are you suggesting we stop when we've just discovered the trail? We've finally heard of a sighting of Moby-Dick!"

"If we don't stop, sir," Starbuck said, "we'll lose more oil in a day than we might gather in a year."

"I am not going to waste time with a petty thing like that," Ahab said.

"We've sailed twenty thousand miles for this," Starbuck tried to explain.

"We're not there yet," Ahab scoffed.

"I am talking about oil, sir," Starbuck said.

"And I most certainly am not!" Ahab said very sternly. "Please leave me now. I cannot be bothered with this."

"Sir," Starbuck said. His face was getting red.

He was trying to not lose his temper. "I can't agree with your line of thinking."

"I am the captain of this ship!" Ahab said. "That means *I* am in charge. That means *I* am the lord and master of this ship. Now get back on deck and leave me to my duties!"

Starbuck turned and went back up to the deck. I followed, but not before I saw Ahab start to pace about his room.

"How dare he speak to me like that," he muttered to himself. "I should punish him. I could make sure that he never gets another first-mate job again!"

Ahab made his way back up to the deck. He watched his crew working away.

Starbuck was directing us men back down into the hold. We were going to mend the leak ourselves rather than stop for repairs.

Ahab realized that he had won the fight. "I suppose you did listen when I gave my command," he said to himself. "Ah, Starbuck," he said. "Perhaps you are too honest a fellow."

Ahab then called out to his crew. "Pull up the anchor! Set up the high sails! We're moving along."

Everyone did just as Ahab commanded. The *Pequod* set off again in search of the white whale.

We continued our search through the casks of oil to discover the leak. The newer ones were fine. It had to be the older ones tucked in farther. We dug deep and continued in our hunt.

It was dark and cold and very wet in the hold. Unfortunately Queequeg, my dearest friend, took ill as a result. He got a terrible fever from working down there.

We placed him in his hammock with blankets to protect him from his chill. He quickly wasted away. Dark circles formed under his eyes. He had trouble focusing on us as we tended to him. We all thought he was reaching his end.

He called me to his side one day and asked

a favor. When he was in Nantucket, he had seen some canoes made of dark wood. The man selling them said whalers were buried in them. He would like to be buried in similar canoe.

I did not want to talk about his death, but Queequeg insisted. "These are things you should know," he said.

So, the carpenter set to work building Queequeg a canoe.

When it was done, Queequeg asked to see it. Then he asked that someone get his harpoon. He had the spear placed inside his canoe along with a paddle from his boat. A piece of sailcloth was rolled up for a pillow.

Queequeg asked to be lifted into the canoe. He wanted to rest inside. Then everyone waited. We all thought that Queequeg would die quietly in this pose.

Nothing happened. Queequeg just lay there with his eyes closed. So, we returned him to his hammock. And then, after all this work, Queequeg began to improve.

Within a few days, he was back to normal. He suddenly leaped to his feet, threw his arms out, and danced a quick jig. He did not let his canoe go to waste, though. He used it as a sea chest and kept all of his belongings inside.

It was only a day or two after Queequeg recovered that we met another ship, the *Rachel*.

As always, Captain Ahab pulled the *Pequod* alongside her. He asked the crew if they had seen the white whale.

"Yes," their captain replied. "We saw him just yesterday."

Ahab could barely contain his excitement! He wanted to race to the deck of his ship and start the search right away.

"Where was he?" Ahab stammered. "Not killed. Not killed, I hope."

The captain quickly told their story. The

crew of *Rachel* had been giving chase to a pod of whales when Moby-Dick suddenly appeared before them. The waves surrounded their boats, and Moby-Dick's flapping, monstrous tail made it more difficult to stay afloat.

Then one of the boats disappeared in the commotion. They did not know if it went down or if it was lost at sea.

"We need your help," the captain of the *Rachel* said. "Please help us find our missing boat. We don't want to lose our men."

Ahab did his best to avoid the topic. He wanted to look for the white whale, not a lost boat. He turned the *Pequod* away from the *Rachel* without saying good-bye or good luck.

That night, while most of us slept and some were left on duty, we heard the cry.

"There she blows!" a voice called from the masthead. "And it's Moby-Dick! Moby-Dick is coming up for air."

CHAPTER 18

The First Day

ᴄᴏ

"Boats! Boats!" cried Captain Ahab. "Get into your boats, men!" The captain shouted his orders while climbing down from the upper deck. He was at the side of the ship in only a few quick steps.

Soon all the boats but Starbuck's were in the water. The sea was smooth and calm. It was like a carpet laid out before them. All the men rowed swiftly, but they approached their target with care. Captain Ahab's boat was in the front.

They were so close to the white whale that

they could see his hump gliding smoothly through the water. Captain Ahab was breathless. He could see the whale's wrinkled head poking out of the sea. It was a beautiful sight.

Bubbles danced alongside Moby-Dick's head as he passed through the water. Birds hovered over the white whale's back. They swooped down to the water then back up into the sky.

Sticking straight out of the whale's back was a long harpoon. It was another reminder of a hunter who had fought against the whale and lost.

I understood how Moby-Dick could draw so many men who believed they could conquer and capture this beast. At this moment, the whale was easy to approach. Moby-Dick looked gentle. This was a lie.

Moby-Dick, at long last, lifted himself up from the water. He arched his tremendous body into a perfect curve. He revealed his enormous head and terrifying jaw. Then the whale crashed back into the water, spraying foam across the approaching boats, and dove back under.

The men in the boats held their oars up. They were ready to drop them into the water and start rowing at their captain's call. Everyone waited for Moby-Dick to reappear.

One of the men pointed to the sky. "The birds," he called. "The birds."

All the birds were suddenly flying toward Ahab's boat. They were making joyous cries. The birds could already see what was about to happen.

The sea began to swell. Ahab looked down. There was a white spot far beneath his boat. It grew larger and larger. The white spot became a giant mass beneath the boat. It turned to the side and showed two terrifying rows of teeth to Ahab. It was Moby-Dick rising from the bottom. His mouth was open, and he was preparing to swallow Ahab's boat.

Ahab grabbed an oar from one of the men and quickly turned the vessel. He then made his way to the front, picked up a harpoon, and took his position. He told his men to get ready. They should start rowing at his command.

This move should have put them beside the whale's head when he reached the surface. Moby-Dick must have realized this, however, for he moved to follow Ahab. The white whale rolled over and rose to the surface, underbelly first. His mouth was opened wide. His lower jaw rose over the boat, and Moby-Dick tried to bite down.

One of his teeth barely missed Ahab as it clamped into one end of the boat. The white whale held it tightly in his mouth, then shook it like a cat would shake a mouse. The men tried to escape his jaws by moving to one end of the boat. That is, all of the men except Ahab. He kept to his spot at the front.

The men could not go very far, though. The boat was small, especially when compared with the whale's enormous jaw. The men tried to hit him with oars and harpoons. It was impossible to get a good shot. They could not reach around his jaw. Too much of the boat was in the whale's mouth.

Their boat was starting to break up around them. Ahab used oars and the harpoon to stab at the whale. He beat with all his fury but had no success. The small boat snapped in two.

All the men landed in the water. They swam back together and clung to half of the wreck. They bobbed up and down in the waves.

Ahab was thrown face-first into the water. He sank beneath the surface.

The white whale moved away from the wreckage. He swam a short distance from them. The top part of his head was so large that it rose twenty feet above the surface. The waves bounced against him as he waited.

Then he started to swim again. He circled the wreckage and the crew. He was so powerful that he began to form a whirlpool.

Ahab was struggling in the water. It was difficult for him to swim with one leg. His men were clinging to the wrecked boat and could not get to him. The other whaleboats, including the one I was on, were unharmed. We all witnessed the entire scene and wanted desperately to help the captain. But it was impossible to cross the path the whale made. His circles started getting smaller and smaller. All of the men were trapped in the middle.

Ahab shouted to the men still on the *Pequod*.

"Sail on!" he shouted. "Sail—" A giant wave washed over him and cut off his speech.

"Sail on the whale!" he called. "Drive him off!"

The *Pequod* did just that. She sailed into the whale's circular path and cut him off. Moby-Dick swam away, and the whaleboats moved in for the rescue.

Stubbs dragged Captain Ahab into his boat. My boat had already arrived back at the *Pequod*. Queequeg and I leaned on the railing of the ship to watch Ahab's rescue. The old man lay on the bottom of Stubbs's boat, broken and bruised. He called Stubbs to him.

"Where is the harpoon?" he asked. "Did we lose the harpoon?"

"No, sir," Stubbs replied. "We have it right here."

"Good, good." Ahab sighed. "Place it with me, please."

Stubbs laid the harpoon on Ahab's chest.

"And the men?" Ahab asked. "Did we lose any men?"

Stubbs shook his head. "None, sir," he said. "They are all right here."

"Help me up," Ahab said. "I want to stand."

Stubbs and another man helped their captain stand up. He looked out in the direction that Moby-Dick swam.

"Look," Ahab shouted. "I can see him now. That's his spout sending spray from the sea. That's all I needed!" he shouted. "I have my strength back! Get your oars ready. Arm the harpoons! We are back in this fight."

The white whale, however, was still swimming away with great speed. It was too great for a small boat powered by oars. There was no way they could keep up.

So, the two remaining boats were lifted back on to the *Pequod* and the great ship took chase. In no time at all we were following the foamy path of the white whale.

The men in the mastheads watched for signs of Moby-Dick. Whenever one could see the white mass breaking the surface, he called to the crew. He also let them know when the whale dove under.

Ahab paced back and forth on the deck, waiting for Moby-Dick to surface again. He was extremely agitated. He counted the minutes until an hour was up. An hour was as long as a whale could last underwater. As soon as that last second was counted, he called to the crew.

"Has anyone seen him?" Ahab called. "Will anyone win the doubloon?"

When the answer came back as no, Ahab became more depressed. He would not leave the deck. He stared into the water, waiting. Waiting for some kind of sign.

The waiting continued through the night and into the next day.

CHAPTER 19

The Second Day

⌒

At dawn, the men in the mastheads changed shifts. There was no telling how far the whale had traveled. We didn't know if we were still on his trail.

Just when we were starting to lose hope, Moby-Dick burst into view.

The great white whale leaped into the air and crashed back down into the water. It was a majestic sight but one that frightened many of the men. We had already seen what Moby-Dick could do.

"I hope you know that you have met your doom!" Captain Ahab shouted to the whale. "Our men are ready. Our harpoon is ready. This will be the end of you!"

Three boats were lowered into the water this time. Queequeg got into one, and I got into another. Starbuck remained on board the *Pequod*.

"The ship is yours, Starbuck," Captain Ahab said. "Keep it away from the boats but don't go too far."

The boats were in the water only a few moments—with Ahab taking the center—when Moby-Dick charged toward us. The whale picked up tremendous speed. He swam with his mouth wide open and his tail lashing about.

All of the men in these boats were expert sailors. Now that we knew what to expect, we understood how to keep away from the beast. We twisted and turned the boats and kept our distance from the angry whale. Ahab shouted encouragement to everyone. He promised us we would win. We *would* kill Moby-Dick. Ahab was not going to let the whale take charge again.

While the boats moved toward and away from the whale, the harpooners were able to strike him with their spears. As each one sank in, we all cheered. However, this did not slow the whale down.

Since a rope was attached to each harpoon, a lot of line passed among the boats. As Moby-Dick darted toward the boats and the boats darted away from him, the lines became tangled.

The situation was becoming more and more dangerous. Ahab's boat was trapped amid all the lines. It was locked into place and could not move.

Ahab did the only thing possible. He began to cut some of the lines. There was no other way to free his boat.

The white whale dove deep again then shot back up to the surface. This time, he caught the bottom of Ahab's boat with his nose and sent it flying. Ahab and his crew crashed into the ocean.

Moby-Dick, once again, dove under and swam away, leaving the sea quiet for the time being.

The *Pequod* moved in closer and pulled all the men to safety.

Captain Ahab needed help to walk around the deck. Many of the men gasped when they saw him, but no one said a word. His ivory leg had broken off. He was left only with a small splinter.

Ahab paused long enough to demand a crutch. After that, he began calling to the men to stand guard near their whaleboats. He shouted for the sails to be raised to move the *Pequod* faster through the water. "We're close, men! We'll soon have that creature!"

Starbuck had finally had enough. He could not watch the crew be put into danger anymore. They had been on high alert for almost two days, and they needed a rest.

"The answer is *never*, old man!" Starbuck yelled. "You will never catch the whale this way. This chase has lasted two days. We've lost two boats. You've lost your leg again. What are you waiting for? Will you finally stop when every one of your men has been killed?"

We were all amazed to hear Starbuck speak like this to his captain. It was unheard of! A sailor must never yell at his superior. He must do exactly as he is told or it is considered treason. We all expected Ahab to punish Starbuck or order that we take him into custody. The captain, however, spoke calmly.

"We can't stop now," Ahab said. "This is a matter of fate. This whale is my destiny. You are my crew so this is your destiny, too."

The man keeping watch in the main masthead called out to everyone below.

"He's swimming alongside us!" he called. He pointed to a white mass to the left of the ship. Moby-Dick kept pace with the *Pequod* for several miles. He then disappeared below the waves again.

CHAPTER 20

The End

On the third day, we finally had another chance to capture the whale. Ahab insisted he could take charge of a boat despite his missing leg. He would not let anything slow him down.

As the boat was about to be lowered, Ahab called to Starbuck. "Many men don't survive battles like this," he said.

"Yes, sir," Starbuck said. "That's very true."

"Starbuck," he said. "I am an old man. Shake hands with me, man."

Starbuck took his captain's hand and gave it a tight squeeze. "Oh, my captain," he said. "Please reconsider this! Stay here on board the *Pequod* with us."

Ahab let go of his first mate's hand. He ordered that the boat be lowered.

Starbuck then noticed another danger. "Sharks," he called. "Come back, sir! There are sharks approaching."

Ahab heard nothing. He was already rowing away and calling orders to the men. He was trying to get his boat close to the white whale.

There was a cry from above. The man sitting in the masthead was shouting to Ahab. The whale was rising in the water beneath them. Ahab moved his boat, hoping that he would place them in the best position to strike with harpoons.

Moby-Dick shot out of the water and crashed

back into the sea. His body was covered with lances and harpoons, old and new. Ropes trailed after him.

The waves from Moby-Dick's crashing body rocked all of the boats, but everyone stayed upright.

Starbuck watched all these events unfold. "Oh, Captain," he said to himself. "If only you would give up this terrible mission. Why can't you realize that the whale does not care about you. He is not chasing you. Only you are chasing him."

Ahab continued on. The three harpooners, including Queequeg, took up positions in the mastheads. Other men took up posts near the railing.

The captain was at long last able to get close to the whale. He shot his harpoon and it landed solidly in the great creature's chest. The whale rolled over several times, trying to

remove himself from Ahab's harpoon and rope. As he rolled over, he almost took Ahab and his boat with him.

Ahab's men used their oars to quickly move the boat to a safer spot. They had to dart back and forth a few times until they were out of harm's way. The white whale swam off and waited for them. He rested only a short distance away.

All of the men on the *Pequod* could see what was going to happen next. The men in the mastheads tried to warn Ahab. But he could see or hear nothing except the whale in front of him.

The whale dashed forward again. He swam at a great speed. The captain made another great shot and pierced the beast with another harpoon.

Ahab glanced to the *Pequod*. Starbuck was leaning over the rail. The first mate looked very

concerned. Other crew members were preparing to drag the great whale back to their ship.
Everyone looked tired and drained of energy.
Their bodies were moving, but their eyes seemed
asleep.

Even the great whale seemed to be slowing.
Perhaps the three-day chase was finally wearing
him down. Only the surrounding sharks seemed
energized.

"I wonder," the captain said to himself. "I
wonder if the sharks are waiting for the whale
or for me?"

And then, without another thought, Ahab
sank another spear into the whale.

Moby-Dick groaned and rolled on his side.
As he turned, he swept against Ahab's boat and
almost turned it over.

The captain was able to grab hold of a beam
and not fall in the water. Three of his men were
not so lucky. They were tossed overboard, but

managed to stay afloat.

Ahab's boat was nearly destroyed. He had lost some of his men. Ropes and harpoons were scattered on the boat's floor.

The *Pequod* was coming in closer to help. The rest of the crew intended to pick up the men who fell overboard and help Ahab back onto the ship.

Moby-Dick turned toward the large ship. He raised his head slightly above water as though he was noticing the ship for the first time. Perhaps he decided that the *Pequod* was the cause of all his troubles. He paused for a moment then charged toward her.

Ahab and his men saw the whale take off toward their ship. They tried to do anything to prevent a disaster. They rowed as fast as they could—they shouted to the men on board – but it was useless.

The white whale rammed against the ship

with all his might. The quake knocked everyone on board to the deck. They picked themselves up right away and tried to make it to the rail. They needed to be ready to cast a rope or harpoon if necessary.

Moby-Dick smashed against the ship again and knocked them all down once more.

They got to the rail and readied their harpoons and lances. They waited, weapons poised, for the whale to reveal himself.

He was under the ship, though. He rammed his head against the bottom of the *Pequod.* All of the men heard a great crack as the bottom of the ship came apart. Moby-Dick had wrecked the *Pequod.* The ship was sinking!

While Moby-Dick smashed his body against the ship, Ahab took aim one more time and shot. The harpoon pierced the whale's flesh and Moby-Dick let out a terrible moan.

The whale rose up from the water, his head

rising high above the sinking masthead. He crashed back into the water and went under.

The rope attached to the last harpoon followed after the whale. Ahab did not seem to realize that the rope was tangled. It spun wildly out of the boat after the harpoon and wrapped itself around Ahab's neck. Even before the captain could call out, he was yanked from the boat and dragged down after the whale.

At first, the crew remaining in his boat stood still. Everyone was stunned. When they turned back to look at the *Pequod*, they faced an even bigger surprise. Nothing was left of the ship except the top part of her mast. They watched as she continued to tip, then sink under the waves forever.

Then, in the swirling waters created by the sinking *Pequod*, Ahab's whaleboat—the last boat—was pulled down, too. It followed the

Pequod into the doomed waters.

You might ask where I was during all of this. I was with Ahab in his boat. I watched from a distance of few feet as he was dragged down with the whale.

I was the only survivor of the *Pequod*. Everyone else went down with the ship or the last whaleboat. I am the only one left to tell this tale of Captain Ahab and Moby-Dick.

As the whaleboat was pulled under by the force of the sinking *Pequod*, several of us tried to swim away. I was the only one to make it to a safe distance. There was nothing left and I had no more chances. I assumed that I would soon drown, too. Or that the sharks would soon find me.

Then I saw a wooden box shoot out from the water. It landed quietly then floated toward me. It was Queequeg's coffin.

I climbed inside and floated for three days.

Eventually I was picked up. It was the crew of the *Rachel* that found me. They were still out looking for their lost whaleboat and the missing men.

I thought it was peculiar that the *Rachel* was out looking for her lost children, but all they found was me—yet another orphan.

What Do *You* Think?
Questions for Discussion

‿ᴖ

Have you ever been around a toddler who keeps asking the question "Why?" Does your teacher call on you in class with questions from your homework? Do your parents ask you questions about your day at the dinner table? We are always surrounded by questions that need a specific response. But is it possible to have a question with no right answer?

The following questions are about the book you just read. But this is not a quiz! They are designed to help you look at the people, places, and events in the stories from different angles. These questions do not have specific answers. Instead, they might make you think of the stories in a completely new way.

Think carefully about each question and enjoy discovering more about this classic story.

1. Ishmael goes to sea not only for work, but for adventure. Do you think he gets to experience this? Have you ever had an adventure?

2. What is the relationship between Ishmael and Queequeg? Do you think it's a solid friendship? How do you think they feel about each other? Do you have good friends who are different from you?

3. Ishmael hears a lot about Captain Ahab before he ever sees him. What does he think when Ahab comes to the deck for the first time? What does Ahab look like? Is there someone in your life who made a big first impression?

4. Does Captain Ahab seem like a good leader to you? What parts of his personality make him well-suited to being the captain of a ship? Do you think you have qualities to become a good leader?

5. How does Ishmael react when he first sees Moby-Dick? How would you have reacted? Does Moby-Dick live up to the legends and stories about him?

6. Starbuck, Stubbs, and Flask are important crew members on the *Pequod*. What do they do to make sure the voyage is running smoothly? Have you ever had to work in a team to get a job done?

7. Captain Ahab stays in his cabin for days at a time. What do you think he does in there? What do you think the captain's cabin looks like?

8. Starbuck says that Moby-Dick isn't chasing Captain Ahab, but that Ahab is chasing the white whale. Do you agree with this? Can you

remember a time when you wanted something so badly you'd do anything to get it?

9. Do you think it was right for Starbuck to stand up to Captain Ahab? Would you have stood up for what you believe or would you have obeyed your captain?

10. If you were a part of a whale ship crew, what job would you want to have: harpooner, sailor, mate, or captain? Why?

A Note to Parents and Educators
By Arthur Pober, EdD

⌒

First impressions are important.

Whether we are meeting new people, going to new places, or picking up a book unknown to us, first impressions count for a lot. They can lead to warm, lasting memories or can make us shy away from any future encounters.

Can you recall your own first impressions and earliest memories of reading the classics?

Do you remember wading through pages and pages of text to prepare for an exam? Or were you the child who hid under the blanket to read with a flashlight, joining forces with Robin Hood to save Maid Marian? Do you remember only how long it took you to read a lengthy novel such as *Little Women*? Or did you become best friends with the March sisters?

Even for a gifted young reader, getting through long chapters with dense language can easily become overwhelming and can obscure the richness of the story and its characters. Reading an abridged, newly crafted version of a classic novel can be the gentle introduction a child needs to explore the characters and storyline without the frustration of difficult vocabulary and complex themes.

Reading an abridged version of a classic novel gives the young reader a sense of independence and the satisfaction of finishing a "grownup" book. And when a child is engaged with and inspired by a classic story, the tone is set for further exploration of the story's themes, characters, history, and details. As a child's reading skills advance, the desire to tackle the original, unabridged version of the story will naturally emerge.

If made accessible to young readers, these stories can become invaluable tools for understanding themselves in the context of their families and social environments. This is why the Classic Starts series includes questions that stimulate discussion regarding the impact and social relevance of the characters and stories today. These questions can foster lively conversations between children and their parents or teachers. When we look at the issues, values, and standards of past times in terms of how we live now, we can appreciate literature's classic tales in a very personal and engaging way.

Share your love of reading the classics with a young child, and introduce an imaginary world real enough to last a lifetime.

Dr. Arthur Pober, EdD

Dr. Arthur Pober has spent more than twenty years in the fields of early childhood and gifted education. He is the former principal of one of the world's oldest laboratory schools for gifted youngsters, Hunter College Elementary School, and former Director of Magnet Schools for the Gifted and Talented for more than 25,000 youngsters in New York City.

Dr. Pober is a recognized authority in the areas of media and child protection and is currently the U.S. representative to the European Institute for the Media and European Advertising Standards Alliance.

Explore these wonderful stories in our
Classic Starts™ library.

20,000 Leagues Under the Sea

The Adventures of Huckleberry Finn

The Adventures of Robin Hood

The Adventures of Sherlock Holmes

The Adventures of Tom Sawyer

Alice in Wonderland & Through the Looking Glass

Animal Stories

Anne of Avonlea

Anne of Green Gables

Arabian Nights

Around the World in 80 Days

Ballet Stories

Black Beauty

The Call of the Wild

Dracula